A Chimney Sweep's Day

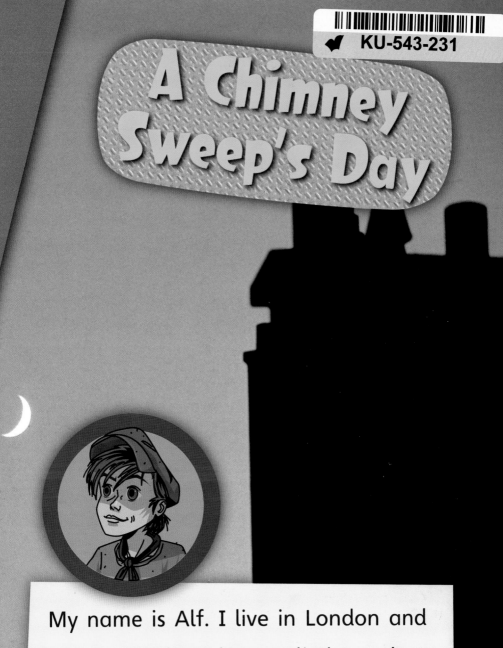

My name is Alf. I live in London and I am a climbing boy. I climb up the inside of chimneys to brush away the soot so that the coal fires burn well.

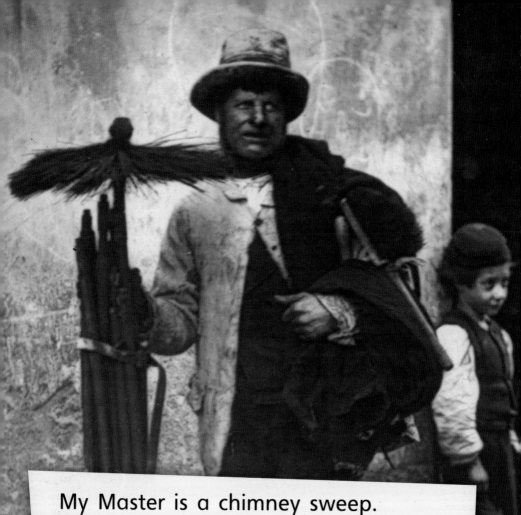

My Master is a chimney sweep.
My parents sold me to him when I was
seven years old. After seven years
I can get another job but what job
could I get? My back is twisted from
climbing up the narrow chimneys.

INTO THE DARK

Contents

Dee Reid

Story illustrated by
Marcelo Baez

Heinemann

Before Reading

Find out about

- Life as a child chimney sweep in Victorian England

Tricky words

- soot
- everywhere
- bruises
- tough
- leather
- suddenly
- carriage
- cellar

Introduce these tricky words and help the reader when they come across them later!

Text starter

Read about Alf, a climbing boy in Victorian England. He climbs up chimneys to brush away the soot so that the coal fires burn well. It is very hard work and very dangerous. Alf started as a climbing boy when he was only seven years old.

I work for my Master six days a week.
On Sundays I go to Sunday School.
The teacher shouts at me because
I get soot on her books.
It's not my fault. I only have a bath
three times a year.

When we get to a house, my Master puts sheets on the carpet to stop the soot getting everywhere. I stand on the sheets and if I see the owners of the house I have to bow my head.

Then I take off my clothes so I can fit into the narrow chimney.

When I first started going up chimneys, I got bruises on my knees and elbows. But now my skin is as tough as leather.

As I start to climb up the chimney, soot falls on my head and then covers all my body. When I look up, soot falls into my eyes and makes them sting.

It is dark in the chimney and I have to feel my way. All the way up I am brushing the soot away and hoping that I can find a way out at the top.

One time, I got stuck in a chimney. I could hear my Master shouting from far below telling me to hurry up or he would light a fire under me.

I made myself as thin as possible
and slowly pushed myself up.
I left most of the skin from my knees
and elbows in that chimney.

Another time I climbed up and up, and then, suddenly, I was at the top of the chimney. I looked far below and I saw a gold carriage going by. It was Queen Victoria on her way to Buckingham Palace!

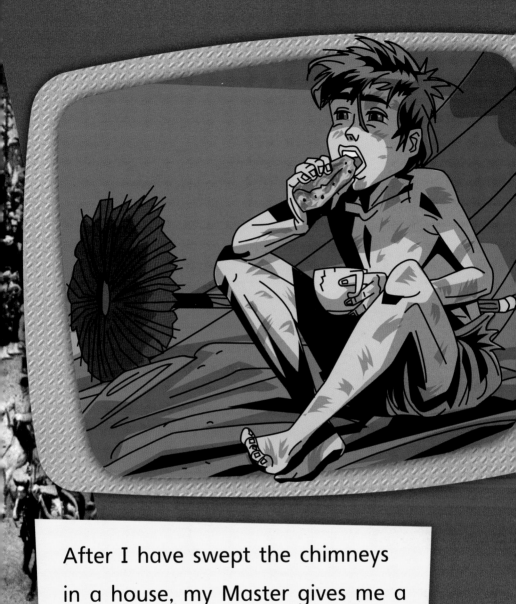

After I have swept the chimneys in a house, my Master gives me a crust of bread and a cup of beer. The bread gets covered in soot but I eat it anyway.

At the end of the day I am so tired I can hardly walk home. My Master gives me a bowl of thin soup to eat. Then I sleep in the cellar on bags of soot. Tomorrow, I will be up the chimneys again.

Quiz

Text Detective

- What did the Master do to make Alf climb more quickly?
- What do you think would be the worst part of being a climbing boy?

Word Detective

- **Phonic Focus:** Identifying long- and short-vowel phonemes

  Page 9: How many syllables are there in the word 'hoping'? Is the vowel phoneme in each syllable long or short?
- Page 3: Find two different words that are plural.
- Page 7: What is Alf's skin compared to? Why is it a good comparison?

Super Speller

Read these words:

started slowly tomorrow

Now try to spell them!

HA! HA! HA!

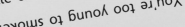

Q What did the big chimney say to the little chimney?

A You're too young to smoke!

In this story

 Scott

 Ben

 The Master

Introduce these tricky words and help the reader when they come across them later!

Tricky words

- mirror
- wearing
- clothes
- fireplace
- passages
- soot
- diamond
- gleam

Story starter

Scott's gran had found an old mirror in her attic. She gave it to Scott and he hung it up on his bedroom wall. But when Scott looked in the old mirror, something very strange happened – the boy in the mirror wasn't Scott!

Scott and the Sweep

Scott looked in the old mirror.

Someone looked back at him.

The boy in the mirror looked a bit like Scott but he wasn't Scott and he was wearing very strange clothes.

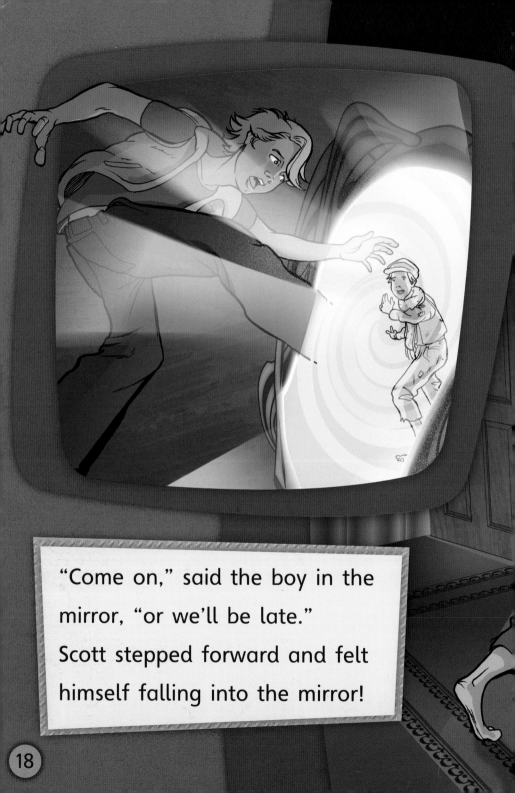

"Come on," said the boy in the mirror, "or we'll be late."
Scott stepped forward and felt himself falling into the mirror!

Scott looked around. He was standing by a fireplace in an old house.

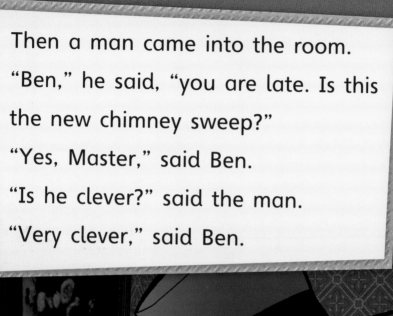

Then a man came into the room.

"Ben," he said, "you are late. Is this the new chimney sweep?"

"Yes, Master," said Ben.

"Is he clever?" said the man.

"Very clever," said Ben.

"Why is he wearing such strange clothes?" asked the man.

"I don't know," said Ben.

"Well, come on," said the man, "we have work to do."

"We have to climb up the chimney and sweep it clean," said Ben.

"I've got a bad feeling about this," thought Scott.

"Hurry up," said the man, "or I'll light this fire and toast you to a crisp!"

"I've got a **very** bad feeling about this," thought Scott.

Ben and Scott started climbing up the chimney. It was very dark and there were lots of passages. Soot got into Scott's ears, his eyes and his mouth.

Just then Scott saw something on a ledge. He reached out and picked it up.

It was covered in black soot. It looked like a piece of glass. Scott wiped it clean. It wasn't glass. It was a diamond – a big, twinkling diamond!

"Come on, Ben," said Scott, "we're getting out of here."

"No!" said Ben. "My Master will kill me if I don't sweep this chimney."

"You don't need to worry about your Master any more," said Scott.

Ben and Scott climbed down the chimney
and came out in a different room.
"You'll never have to climb a dark
sooty chimney again," said Scott.
And he showed Ben the diamond.

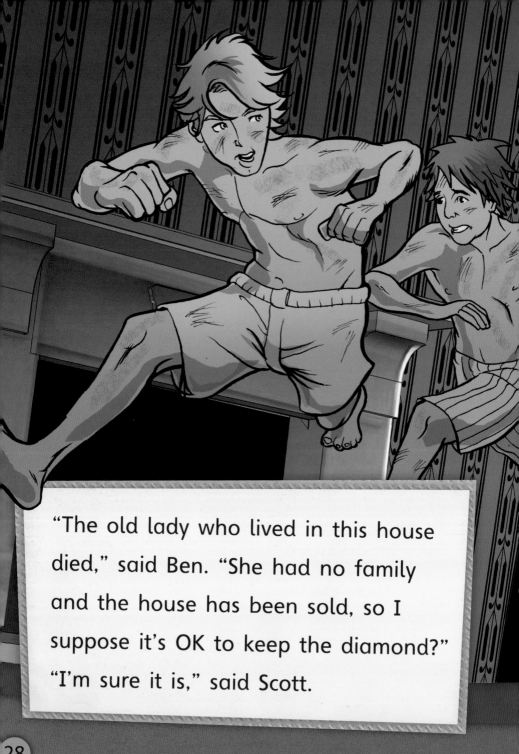

"The old lady who lived in this house died," said Ben. "She had no family and the house has been sold, so I suppose it's OK to keep the diamond?"
"I'm sure it is," said Scott.

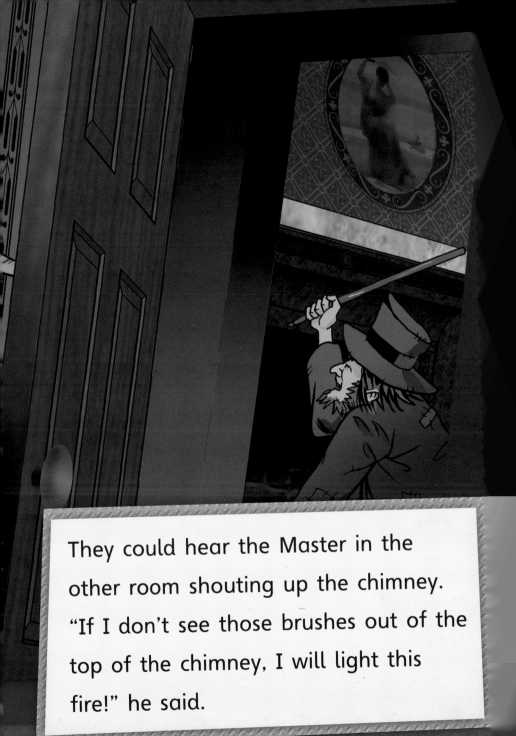

They could hear the Master in the other room shouting up the chimney. "If I don't see those brushes out of the top of the chimney, I will light this fire!" he said.

"I was right," said Ben. "You are clever. You have saved my life."

Just as Scott gave Ben the diamond, something very strange happened. The sun shone on the diamond and made it gleam like a mirror. Scott looked at the diamond and felt himself falling forwards.

Scott was back in his bedroom looking at his old mirror. The person looking back at Scott was Scott!

"Strange," thought Scott as he brushed some soot from his jumper.

Quiz

Text Detective

- Why will Ben never have to climb chimneys again?
- What do you think the Master will do when he realises that Ben has run off?

Word Detective

- **Phonic Focus:** Identifying long- and short-vowel phonemes

  Page 31: How many syllables are there in the word 'bedroom'? Is the vowel phoneme in each syllable long or short?
- Page 25: Which two adjectives describe the diamond?
- Page 26: Which words are contracted in the word 'we're'?

Super Speller

Read these words:

sweep   clever   we're

Now try to spell them!

HA! HA! HA!

Q What can go up the chimney down, but not down the chimney up?

A An umbrella!